HELLO MY NAME IS

BOB

BY LINAS ALSENAS

Scholastic Press | New York

Library of Congress Cataloging-in-Publication Data Available.

ISBN-13 978-0-545-05244-3
ISBN-10 0-545-05244-0

10 9 8 7 6 5 4 3 2 1 09 10 11 12 13 14

Printed in Singapore 46
First edition, February 2009

The text type was set in Coop Forge.
Book design by Phil Falco

My name is Bob.
I'm a bear.
But I should warn you,

I'm very boring.

HELLO
BOB

You really shouldn't bother reading this book.

You'll be totally bored by the end.

Some bears like to chase each other and play

games and travel and do all kinds of stuff.
GRIN AND BEAR IT

Not me.
I like to stay home.
Sometimes I count
toothpicks.

Or practice humming.

But mostly, I just sit.

And sit.

And sit.

Sitting's great, isn't it?

This is my friend Jack.

He's not boring at all.

He's always doing wacky stuff.

Wild stuff!

CRAZY stuff!!

Not me, though. I like being at home.
Dusting the plants.

Knitting.

If I'm feeling zany, I might go for a slow walk outside.

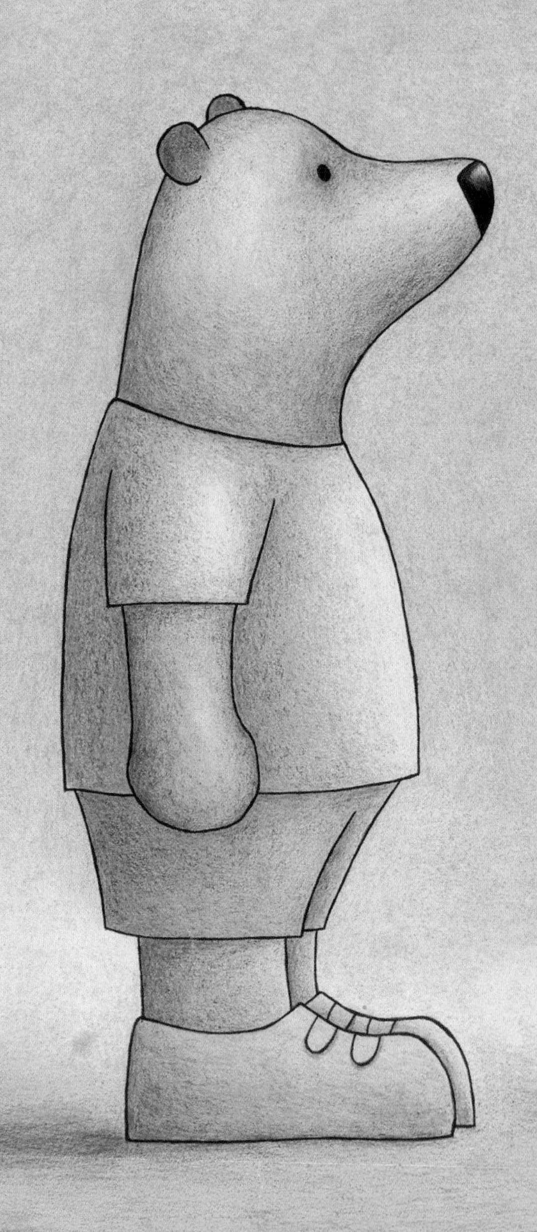

I like the moon.
It's pretty.

Sometimes Jack takes
me to his favorite places,
like the **ice cream shop.**

Or the **alligator swamp.**

Or the amusement park!

Other times, I take Jack
to **my** favorite places.

Like the parking lot.

Or the laundry room.

Or the couch.

Sitting is so great.

It's amazing how two bears
who are so different can be friends.
But we like it that way.

And you know, at the end of the day,
we're not **that** different.
Jack can be boring, just like me.

Especially when
he falls asleep.